THE CAZUELA

THAT THE FARM MAIDEN STIRRED

SAMANTHA R. VAMOS

ILLUSTRATED BY RAFAEL LÓPEZ

Charlesbridge

For Jackson and my father, with love,
and with gratitude to *mi amiga querida,* Rosamaria—S. R. V.

To Richard and Sylvia, for soul-stirring *consejos*—R. L.

Text copyright © 2011 by Samantha R. Vamos
Illustrations copyright © 2011 by Rafael López
All rights reserved, including the right of reproduction in whole or in part in any form.
Charlesbridge and colophon are registered trademarks of Charlesbridge Publishing, Inc.

Published by Charlesbridge
85 Main Street
Watertown, MA 02472
(617) 926-0329
www.charlesbridge.com

Library of Congress Cataloging-in-Publication Data
Vamos, Samantha R.
    The cazuela that the farm maiden stirred / Samantha R. Vamos ;
illustrations by Rafael López.
        p. cm.
    Summary: A cumulative tale of a farm maiden who, aided by a group of animals, prepares
"Arroz con Leche," or rice pudding. Includes recipe and glossary of the Spanish words that
are woven throughout the text.
    ISBN 978-1-58089-242-1 (reinforced for library use)
[1. Cookery—Fiction. 2. Domestic animals—Fiction. 3. Spanish language—Vocabulary.]
I. López, Rafael, 1961– ill. II. Title.
PZ7.V2565Caz 2011
[E]—dc22   2010007547

Printed in Singapore
(hc) 10 9 8 7 6 5 4 3 2 1

Illustrations painted in acrylics on grained wood
Display type and text type set in Posada and Goudy
Color separations by Chroma Graphics, Singapore
Printed and bound September 2010 by Imago in Singapore
Production supervision by Brian G. Walker
Designed by Susan Mallory Sherman

THIS IS THE POT that the farm maiden stirred.

This is the butter
that went into the **CAZUELA** that the farm maiden stirred.

This is the goat
that churned the cream
to make the **MANTEQUILLA**
that went into the **CAZUELA** that the farm maiden stirred.

This is the cow
that made the fresh milk
while teaching the **CABRA**
that churned the **CREMA**
to make the **MANTEQUILLA**
that went into the **CAZUELA** that the farm maiden stirred.

This is the duck
that went to the market
to buy the sugar
to flavor the **LECHE**
made fresh by the **VACA**
while teaching the **CABRA**
that churned the **CREMA**
to make the **MANTEQUILLA**
that went into the **CAZUELA** that the farm maiden stirred.

This is the donkey
that plucked the lime
and carried the **PATO**
that went to the **MERCADO**
to buy the **AZÚCAR**
to flavor the **LECHE**
made fresh by the **VACA**
while teaching the **CABRA**
that churned the **CREMA**
to make the **MANTEQUILLA**
that went into the **CAZUELA** that the farm maiden stirred.

This is the hen
that laid the eggs
while grating the **LIMÓN**
plucked by the **BURRO**
that carried the **PATO**
that went to the **MERCADO**
to buy the **AZÚCAR**
to flavor the **LECHE**
made fresh by the **VACA**
while teaching the **CABRA**
that churned the **CREMA**
to make the **MANTEQUILLA**
that went into the **CAZUELA** that the farm maiden stirred.

This is the farmer
who planted the rice
while tending the GALLINA
that laid the HUEVOS
while grating the LIMÓN
plucked by the BURRO
that carried the PATO
that went to the MERCADO
to buy the AZÚCAR
to flavor the LECHE
made fresh by the VACA
while teaching the CABRA
that churned the CREMA
to make the MANTEQUILLA
that went into the CAZUELA
that the farm maiden stirred.

When the **MANTEQUILLA** from the **CABRA**,
the **LECHE** from the **VACA**,
the **AZÚCAR** from the **PATO**,
the **LIMÓN** from the **BURRO**,
the **HUEVOS** from the **GALLINA**,
and the **ARROZ** from the **CAMPESINO**
were all mixed in the **CAZUELA**,

the **CABRA** gave out spoons,
the **GALLINA** sang a tune,
the **PATO** beat a **TAMBOR,**
the **BURRO** plucked a banjo,
the **VACA** shook a **MARACA,**
and the **CAMPESINO** and the farm maiden danced . . .

. . . and no one watched the **CAZUELA** that the farm maiden stirred.

The **CAZUELA** simmered and sputtered.

It bubbled and burbled.

Just when it was about to burst,
the farm maiden cried, "Ay!"—

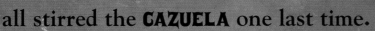

and the **CABRA, VACA, PATO, BURRO, GALLINA, CAMPESINO,** and farm maiden all stirred the **CAZUELA** one last time.

When the **CAZUELA** was finally ready,
everyone said **GRACIAS** for
the **ARROZ CON LECHE** that the **CAMPESINA** stirred.

Arroz con Leche

Rice pudding

Note: This recipe requires the use of a hot stove and should be made with adult assistance and supervision.

Ingredients

1 cup long-grain white rice, uncooked
2 cups whole milk
2 cups heavy cream
$1/3$ cup sugar
2 tablespoons unsalted butter
1 cinnamon stick (extras for garnish if desired)
zest of 1 lime*
2 large egg yolks
ground cinnamon
ground nutmeg (optional)

Equipment

measuring cup(s) and spoons
colander
1 medium and 1 large saucepan
1 stirring spoon and 1 slotted spoon
zester or grater
whisk
small bowl
serving bowl(s) (either 1 large or 6 small individual
  nonmetal bowls)
plastic wrap or aluminum foil

*In Mexico, *limón* refers to a small, green fruit, similar to the
 limes found in the United States. However, in many other
 Spanish-speaking countries, it refers to the larger, yellow lemon.
 You can use either limes or lemons in *arroz con leche*. Both taste delicious!

1. **POUR** the rice into a colander and rinse it with cold water. Thoroughly strain the rice to remove excess water.

2. **HEAT** the milk to boiling in a medium saucepan. Stir in the rice. When the milk has reached a boil again, cover the saucepan and reduce the heat to low for 15 to 20 minutes. The rice should simmer until most, but not all, of the milk is absorbed. Continue to the next step, but take the rice off the heat when it finishes cooking.

3. While the rice is cooking, **COMBINE** the heavy cream, sugar, butter, cinnamon stick, and lime zest in a large saucepan and bring the mixture to a simmer. Stir frequently over medium to medium-low heat for approximately 20 to 25 minutes as the cream mixture begins to thicken. Using a slotted spoon, remove the cinnamon stick. Remove the saucepan from the heat.

4. **STIR** the rice into the cream mixture in the large saucepan.

5. **BEAT** the egg yolks in a small bowl with a whisk. Gradually raise the temperature of the egg yolks by slowly spooning in and whisking 3 tablespoons—one at a time—of the hot rice/cream mixture.

6. **STIR** the egg-yolk mixture into the remaining rice/cream mixture in the large saucepan and heat over low for 2 to 3 minutes.

7. **POUR** the rice pudding into a large nonmetal serving bowl or divide it into 6 individual nonmetal serving bowls. Cover the bowl(s) with plastic wrap or aluminum foil and allow the pudding to cool and thicken in the refrigerator for 30 minutes.

8. **REMOVE** the rice pudding from the refrigerator. Lightly sprinkle the pudding with ground cinnamon before serving. Optional: Sprinkle ground nutmeg and/or garnish each bowl with a cinnamon stick.

RECIPE MAY BE MADE A DAY IN ADVANCE.

GLOSSARY OF SPANISH WORDS

ARROZ (ah-ROHS): rice

ARROZ CON LECHE (ah-ROHS con LEH-cheh): rice pudding

AZÚCAR (ah-SOO-kar): sugar

BURRO (BUR-roh): donkey

CABRA (KAH-brah): goat

CAMPESINA (kam-peh-SEEN-ah): farm maiden

CAMPESINO (kam-peh-SEEN-oh): farmer

CAZUELA (kah-SWAY-lah): pot

CON (CON): with

CREMA (KREM-ah): cream

GALLINA (gah-YEE-nah): hen

GRACIAS (GRAH-see-ahs): thank you

HUEVO (WAY-voh): egg

LECHE (LEH-cheh): milk

LIMÓN (lee-MOHN): lime

MANTEQUILLA (man-teh-KEE-yah): butter

MARACA (mah-RAH-kah): a handheld percussion instrument

MERCADO (mer-KAH-doh): market

PATO (PAH-toh): duck

TAMBOR (tahm-BOR): drum

VACA (VAH-kah): cow